Little Daisy

And

The Sun Stone

Patrick Huet

Copyright

© **Patrick Huet** august 2017

All rights reserved.

Author of the tale : Patrick Huet.

The cover is a composition of Patrick Huet and a picture of Byskt.

Editions Patrick Huet

73 rue Duquesne 69006 Lyon – France.

www.patrick-huet.fr

Tel. (33) 06 99 71 69 69

ISBN : 978-0-244-92900-8

Summary

CHAPTER 01

The mission.

The flat stone leapt over the water, twice ricocheting before landing near a sleepy frog on a large water lily. The frog jumped, frightened and plunged comfortably into the water. A crystalline laugh rose.

Not far away, a little girl laughed cheerfully. She had recently celebrated her twelfth summer, and in her black eyes shone the brilliance of innocence. Her very long and very brown hair was tied with a thin strip of linen with geometric motifs. His dress was simple: a bodice and a fringed suede skirt.

The frog peered curiously out of the water.

Again, the laughter of Little Daisy scattered around sylvery notes.

"Do not be afraid, sister frog, I do not want you any harm. You can go back on the water lily."

The batrachian did not take these declarations into account. It thought it better to go away. When he jumped on the bank in the middle of the reeds, Little Daisy had already forgotten it. She picked up other stones flat enough to ricochet wonderfully over the water. She beat her own record, with a single shot she made more than fifteen rebounds. Never seen ! Even the most skilful boys of his tribe (the Inikawas) had never reached that number.

It's a pity that no one has witnessed his feat !

"I'll come back this afternoon with the other children of the tribe, they will see how clever I am."

At this thought she suddenly remembered the reason for her presence there. There was need of water in the village, if she did not hurry back, she would be rebuked She quickly went out of the brook with the two goatskins filled to the brim, fixed one at each end of a bamboo stem. And she placed it on her shoulder.

The goatskins weighed hard, but his thin body was sturdy. Once standing, she walked with a nimbly step despite the weight of her burden. Before leaving the bank, she turned one last time.

"Good-bye, Sister River. I thank you for your water and shall come back to see you as soon as possible."

It was in the customs of the Inikawas to consider the existing elements as their brother, whether animal, plant or mineral. When they took a part of nature, when they killed an animal for their subsistence, they apologized in advance and thanked him afterwards. So, the reflex of Little Flower of the Field was perfectly natural.

Those the traditions counted for a lot to the Inikawas, especially the Name Ceremony, the moment when the tribe gives a name to a baby.

After the birth of Little Flower of the Field, her parents and the Council of Elders had gathered.

They had been amazed by the extraordinary delicacy of the newborn, who weared the original features of the first immigrants who had settled in the country for a hundred and twenty summers.

These first inhabitants had crossed a considerable distance by land, then an almost limitless ocean before reaching this fertile country. It was said in the evening around the fires that these pioneers fled from the ferocious yoke of a place which they called Atlantis. Over the years, the great air and the sun had browned and reddened the skins. Babies were now born red skin.

Twelve years before, therefore, a newborn broke with this acquired peculiarity. Her skin was so white that it reminded one of the daisy. By mutual agreement, it was called Little Daisy. Season after season, everybody was pleased about the choice of this name. For her look and her dark hair enhanced the brightness of her face. The sun did not turn it brown, quite the reverse, it exalted its opalescence ann its brightness.

At that hour of the morning, as the little girl pushed her way through the tall grass, more than ever she looked like a little flower of the fields.

A circle of about a hundred gray tents protected by a palisade of stakes springs up in front of her. Her village, a tribe of three hundred men, women and children. Above the tepees, a mahogany totem was carved with the effigy of the mascot of the inhabitants: a condor. Wings spread, the large bird seemed to soar. The Inikawas felt reassured by his presence.

Little Daisy turned away from the totem. No one was waiting for her at the entrance of the village. Perhaps she could go to her tepee without being noticed or scolding for her delay.

She advanced, and at once felt an impression of strangeness. She would not have been able to tell what tensed up her nerves and awakened her attention, but her step was slower, her breath shorter and her gaze more acute.

Suddenly, she understood. Not a sound reached

her. The squabbling and laughter of the children had faded, the coughing, the scraping and other sounds emanating from human activities had disappeared. Even the insects had deserted the place; She could no longer hear the buzzing of the bee or the fly. A weight of heavy silence had fallen on the village.

Alarmed, Little Daisy briefly called. The sigh of the breeze was the only answer. From her friends, from her brothers, she obtained nothing but profound silence.

Without letting go of her goatskins, she accelerated her pace and ran, full of apprehension.

She had not crossed the first circle of the tents that she saw them. The surprise nailed her to the floor. All of her tribe were there, infants swaddled in the arms of their mothers and elders clinging to their stick. All without exception were present on the village square, more immobile than statues.

A moan broke the silence and drew Little Daisy Petite Champs from her stillness. She quickly put down her burdens and rushed to the old woman in the center of the circle.

- Mother Of The Tribe ! Mother Of The Tribe, what's going on ? Why do not they move ?

Sitting cross-legged, the white-haired woman gave a heavy look to the little girl. Her tired eyes had known more than a hundred winters, they had witnessed the birth of each of the inhabitants of the village. Therefore everybody rightly called her the Mother of the Tribe. The experience of the many years he had lived had given her wisdom. The intensity of his pupils denied the fragility of her body.

- Listen to me, Little Daisy !

The little girl almost stuck her ear to the eldest woman's lips. The words were barely audible.

- The village is under the rule of a spell. You alone can deliver it.

- But how ?

- Shut up and listen ! Time is running out. In a few moments I would be petrified like the other villagers. Only one thing can break the spell. The

Sun Stone. It lies on the summit of a high mountain towards the west. Go get it !

- How would I recognize it ?

- It is a magic crystal, it takes the color of the sun at every moment of the day. However, he retains his virtues only if he is plucked by an innocent hand and at a specific time in the evening. When the rays dye the crystal with a bright red bright, you will pick it up very quickly, because it will keep its color only ten flutters of eyelashes. And this is the ruby color the village needs. Go, Little Daisy, and came back with the Sun Stone, otherwise we'll remain forever frozen !

The young girl squeezed the stiffened fingers of her grandmother in her hands.

- Mother Of The Tribe, who did this and why ?

In a whisper, she managed to blow.

- Black Soot ! A sorcerer exiled from Atlantis. He wanted to subdue the village to his will, we refused. To take revenge, he cast a spell on us to change us into a stone statue. I have resisted so far, but my body no longer answers. Goodbye Little Daisy ! You alone are free, you alone possess the innocent hand able to pluck the Sunstone. The future of the Inikawas belongs to you.

The old woman's lips stiffened. No more sound was heard.

"Mother Of The Tribe !" Shouted Little Daisy, knowing that all words were useless. Only her actions could bring her back to life as well as the rest of the village. As the Eldest said, the future of the Inikawas was in her hands.

Without a word, without a tear, she stood up. She quickly ran over the familiar faces that surrounded her and then rushed to her tipi before her courage sagged.

The preparations were very fast. Twenty minutes had not passed since her conversation with Mother Of The Tribe that she was at the gates of the village.

A bag of leather stowed on her back contained

food (dried meat and fruit), a leather flask full of water and a blanket. Under a rope around her waist like a belt, she passed a tomahawk and a knife. On her right shoulder a quiver with a dozen arrows. By coquetry, she had adorned her headband with a red and blue eagle feather and her neck with a nacreous necklace pearl (a gift from her grandmother). Her bow slung over her shoulder, she took the start under a sunlight approaching her zenith.

To linger longer at the dead village would have caused her too much trouble; The silence laid a sinister veil on his heart. So she quickly crossed the line, not knowing when she would return, but the mind fixed on her goal. Find the Sun Stone.

Walking intensely did not worry her. Her family were on foot. During the great hunting campaigns of spring and autumn, it was whole days that they traveled thus, weighted down with burdens. In comparison, his equipment today was rather light.

Leaving the village, Little daisy was sad, she was alone in the world and her tribe was dead or almost. After an hour his natural joyfullness took over. It was a warm and beautiful day. The sky, of an extraordinary clarity, was of a porcelain blue. Around her, birds chirped. Their trills accompanied her light step. She eventually imitated them and hummed an improvised air. She soon came to the top of a little hill. She did not touch either her water or her food, preferring to ration in anticipation of future difficulties. Brooks ran here and here the area, she knew, but she had never come to this area and did not know where they were. It was better to spare his water. Food would not be a problem. It was the season of fruits, bushes and shrubs appeared covered with edible berries. Besides, she was skilled at shooting, brother rabbit would provide her with the necessary meat.

The only unknown to her expedition was its length and therefore its duration. The dark eyes of little Inikawas sharpened. She stared at the horizon towards the west. She seemed to perceive a gray tint in the distance like the ethereal veil of a cloud. Was it the mountain indicated by Mother of the Tribe or water vapor rising from the ground ? If it was the mountain, it was at a fantastic distance.

The eyes of Little Daisy wandered over the tremendousgrasslande separating her from this grayish mass. The tall grass waved beneath the breeze, so similar to the water of a pool in times of strong wind. She had never seen the ocean whence her ancestors came, but what she had before her eyes recalled the tales repeatedly told by the ancients. The great meadow was a sea, she would move with little more importance than a fish in the ocean.

His heart suddenly clasped in front of this unknown country. So many terrible stories circulated about those distant areas !

Hunters had one day went to the borders of the territory. They had walked for moons and encountered animals of merciless savagery, gigantic wild beasts. They had reported no evidence of it, so the children had taken their word for boasting. Facing the vast meadow, Little Daisy could not help but think again and feel icy fingers hugging her chest. She shivered in spite of the heat and then recovered. An Inikawas did not let himself be carried away by fear ! She was a free country girl, she would face the great prairie no matter what dangers it contained.

She went down the hill with a firm foot and soon was in the enormous vegetal carpet. The grass came to her shoulder, sometimes it was taller than her head. As she walked forward, it gained more and more in height. Finally, the little girl moved in a grass two meters high. Fortunately, the vegetation was not very dense. The stems were sufficiently spaced to allow her to slip inside as easily as an eel. At times she had to walk around some huges masses of brambles. Their berries were delicious. However, she only picked them after inspection. Wasps or hornets used to build their nests in this kind of bushes and their stings in large numbers did not forgive.

For a long time, she had lost all vision on a large scale. The tall grasses formed a living wall. Had it not been the sun, she would not have known where to direct her steps. So she followed its course far above in the curve of the sky. Wherever he went to bed, she would find the magic crystal, the Sun Ston.

In the evening, when the day was fading, an silvery song rose suddenly: the clear and joyful notes of a running water. She darted forward and soon discovered a refreshing stream. Reeds ran along its banks and surrounded a handful of trees. The place was ideal for the night.

Little Daisy decided to set up camp there.

She uprooted tubers in order to save her provisions as much as possible and then grilled them on a wood fire. The operation required her but a short time. It ignited dry twigs placed under thicker dead branches - thanks to its lighter, a device consisting of two fire stones whose clashes caused sparks. She enjoyed a delicious country meal.

She relaxed in the stream. The fresh water washed her from the dust and tiredness of the journey. Then she rolled herself in her blanket and fell asleep at once, lulled by the murmur of the wind and the brook.

CHAPTER 02

An unexpected encounter

Early before dawn, Little Daisy stood out of his makeshift bed. Life in the open air had no secret for her, the examination of the position of the stars told her that the day would soon rise.

When the first rays of the sun appeared on the east, she had already been on the road for a while and was going at a fast pace.

She went on for several days, walking the whole day on the same rapid pace as her people used to. The perfume of the flowers elated her, the rustling of the leaves rocked her. All trace of fear had disappeared from his soul.

She moved forward her heart full of joy. She did not forget her mission or purpose, but there was no need to lament. Now that her fears had gone, she appreciated every change in the landscape movement. Sister Nature was a pleasant companion, traveling with her was a pleasure, a friend so delightful could not hide dangers.

On the evening of his fifth day, Little daisy had found no streams to quench her thirst. Her leather flask was still three-quarters full, drinking only the bare minimum, she could hold two days. Until then, she would cross a watering point, even if it was tenuous. The future proved him right. The following day, a nonchalant river suddenly unwound its sparkling meanders.

The afternoon was drawing to a close. The moment came to establish her camp there. The river promised to be full of fish. Tonight a carp or a trout would roast at her fire !

She got rid of her things, keeping only her bow. She would fish il the Inikawas way. The fish were fast. She had no chance of catching them only with her fingers.But with an arrow on the other hand ...

She took one of the strands of her rope. She tied one end to the base of an arrow, the other around her wrist. Brother fish could not escape ! She gave him a brief excuse, took off her precious mother-of-pearl necklace and her boots and then entered the middle of the thigh in the river. The water was wetting the bottom of her skirt. It was leather, it would dry quickly.

Little Daisy's sharp eye was trying to break through the waves. The rays of the sun were reflected on the waters and dazzled her.

She was about to change her position when a slight crackle alarmed her. Probably a rodent ! She turned her head, however. Everything seemed normal. The grass swung softly to the wind, a lark landed on a stem and threw himself into a series of trills. Enchanted, Little Daisy smiled at her. Her smile suddenly froze into an expression of stupefaction.

Where her belonginings lay, the space was empty. She rushed forward. In his haste, his foot violently hit a stone in the bed of the river. She fell flat on her stomach. His face disappeared for a moment under the water before reappearing stiffened features.

Half walking, half creeping, Little Daisy climbed on the shore. Feverishly, she looked around her primitive encampment. Perhaps his bag had slipped into the water or elsewhere ? No nothing ! Her things had really disappeared. Bag, ankle boots, as well as tomahawk and mother-of-pearl necklace. An explanation was necessary. It was a theft, and it could only be the act of a human.

She was no longer alone !

The presence of a human being always meant a potential danger, which was repeated many a time to her. The Inikawas were not the only tribe existing on these lands. If to this day no stranger had come to her village during her lifetime****, apart from this wizard of Atlantis, groups of hunters had sometimes met other men during their campaigns. Some were friendly, others frankly hostile. That one of them roamed nearby encouraged Little Daisy to the most extreme vigilance.

She took her breath, tried to slow down the beating of her heart and thought.

Could it have been Black Soot ? For a moment she was afraid of being turned into a stone statue and then reassured herself. If the sorcerer needed anything, he had only to go to the village. Now that he had petrified the inhabitants, their property was at his disposal. It was not her meager things that might have interested him. Moreover, he would not have scuttled away for fear of a girl. No, it was not him !

Traces of tiny footsteps left the bank to get lost in the grass. It was not hers, they were slightly smaller.

- A child ! if she exclaimed. That is why he did not attack me. In the middle of the river and armed with a bow, I had to terrorize him. He preferred to steal and get away. He'll hear me !

Grumbling with rage, she rushed on the trail of

her thief. She uttered a brief cry at once. The ground, strewn with small sharp stones, wounded his feet. The boots made of buffalo leather and reinforced with a soft wooden sole had protected her until then. Barefoot, she could not move as fast as she wanted. Disappointment enraged her, increasing her anger. When she held this child, she would deprive him of the desire to begin again !

Still had to catch him ! At the pace she was advancing, she was not ready to make it.

At this thought, Little Daisy clenched his teeth. She had to join him at all costs. Without her equipment, she would put moons to reach the Suns Sone, if she succeeded. Her boots and his leather flask were more precious than anything else.

The thief's track was incredibly easy to follow. One had to be a pitiful hunter to leave such clues behind him. In the Inikawas, the youngest children were able to move more discreetly, while the older ones made it almost impossible to detect the trace. The child she was pursuing was not a hunter; he knew nothing of the art closely connected with that of dissimulation.

She picked up a strange behavior. Several times the thief suddenly changed direction. She guessed why. In these tall grass, it was difficult to orientate himself, it was a weak point that she decided to exploit.

Depending on the different orientations of the track, she determined the position where he would be most likely to be within the next ten minutes. Then she darted slowly in that direction, keeping her lips clenched so as not to groan under the sharp bite of stones and urticating plants.

Her instinct warned her of a presence even before his ears caught a grunt. Stems were broken, boots hammered on the ground. A smile lit up the face of Little Daisy. For having found her thief in such difficult conditions, she was worthy to be one of the greatest hunters.

Despite the suffering of the soles of her feet, her step became elastic again, her gait supple. At the same time, she nocked an arrow to her bow, ready to fire. Three seconds later, a child's curved back was drawn between the stems. She bent the bow and released it cyrtly. The arrow whistled. It was planted ten centimeters from the right foot of the child.

" No more a gesture where I strike for good ! " She ordered.

As she spoke, she had rearmed her bow. Little Daisy did not want to hurt this child, she just wanted to get her things back. The rest did not concern her, he would be free to wander at his leisure and return to his village. She hoped he would surrender without resistance. If he fled, would she have the courage to shoot him in the back ? No, and that was what bothered her, because in this case she would have lost everything.

Fortunately, he opted for the first solution. He jumped on the spot shouting not to kill him, that he would not move an inch. She conceived some repugnance, no Inikawas would do so ! Confronted with such a situation, he would have remained motionless and would have waited to face his enemy before confronting him. What kind of child was this coward ?

She got her answer as soon as he turned. At once she regretted her curiosity.

The creature before her was not a child. If he had the size, his appearance denied it. He was a gnome with an enormous head and eyes so globular that they seemed exorbitant. His black hair was stuck in greasy wisps on a thick neck. His skin was rough, as if covered with pustules. He was hideous !

Little Daisy repressed a grimace. She stepped forward with a stern look. His eyes fell on the bag held by the gnome, her bag !

"You thief ! You deserve nothing but my arrow in the heart and that I let your carcass rot in the sun.

The gnome threw himself on his knees. He began to groan so horribly that she was tempted to kick him on the ribs to stop these waves of supplications. She was reluctant, however, to touch this bloated body. Exasperated, she ordered him.

- Shut up ! You're just a thief. For having stolen my only thingss, you deserve worse than death.

- Oh ! I implore you, in the name of what is sacred for you, do not kill me ! I am but a little abandoned being, far from his family, lost in this great grassland and condemned to die of hunger.

These last words touched the sensitive heart of Little Daisy. In some ways, this gnome resembled her. He had no tribe left. The globular eyes captured the subtle change of attitude of the little girl, and at once knew how to make it bend. The lamentations resumed, stronger than ever.

Without her having to ask for it, he justified the theft of her belongings.

He was alone in the world, desperate. Ignorant of hunting for food, he was on the brink of famine. Then he saw the bag. Tortured by hunger, he had felt the smell of the food inside and had stolen it. He blamed himself openly. He was guilty and did not deserve mercy. Let her take her life on the spot !

Joining the gesture to the word, he opened his shirt theatrically and offered his bare chest to the vengeful arrow of his pursuer.

Disconcerted by so many groans, Little Daisy was gaping. The wailings of the gnome were so pitiful that she did not notice the sly light in his big, downcast eyes.

She even forgot to question him about the theft of her pretty necklace of pearls and her boots, objects of little interest for someone hungry. She lowered her bow and advanced a step.

- Well ! I am no longer angry. I'm just going to get my business. You're free to go where you want.

With a quick gesture, she picked up her boots and put them on. A smile flourished on her lips when she felt this familiar garment clasp her feet again. How pleasant it would be to walk now ! Her bag was resting beside her. As she leaned over it, she saw the gnome in the corner of her eye moving away in a hurry.

- Hey ! She shouted.

He froze on the spot and turned towards her his voluminous skull

- What is it ? I've given you everything.

Little Daisy shook his head. Her long brown hair waved in her back.

- You forget something.

- What ?

- My necklace.

- Oh !

He seemed sorry. He took the precious jewel out of a pocket of his leather trousers and handed it to the little girl.

- My apologies, young girl, I had forgotten it. I am really sorry.

That he was sorry, his expression proved it amply. As to whether he was sorry for his forgetting or giving back the necklace, there was a difference. Little Daisy did not grasp all the subtlety. She was an expert in the field of hunting, but she did not know the perfidy of certain beings. At this moment the gnome appeared so unhappy that she had a movement of kindness worthy of the noblest sentiments.

- You have not eaten anything for three days, from what I have understood ?

He nodded.

- Join me for tonight, I invite you to share my meal. It will not be said that I shall let someone die of hunger in front of my eyes.

The deformed creature sank into obsequious thanks. Little Daisy did not ask so much. A simple thank you would have be enough. Instead, she had to bear a verbose gloss of which she did not understand half the terms. The words of the gnome had the same effect than a glue.

Cut shorting his speach, she gave the signal for departure and took the direction of her encampment.

Along the way, she inquired about his identity.

- They call me Eye of Toad .

Never had a name been so justly agreed upon by his bearer, she mused. She immediately swept away that thought. It was not respectable to make fun of the appearance of a human brother.

"What are you doing in the great grassland when you do not know how to hunt?"

He brought back a sad story. Warriors from a neighboring tribe had raided his village, killing the able-bodied men, kidnapping children and women to sell them and making them slaves. Little Daisy did not really pictured what slave status was, but imagined it as a terrible thing.

Eye of Toad continued his narrative. The operation against his village had taken place at night. Due to his small size and darkness, he was taken for a child. The next day the aggressors perceived their error, and abandoned it unscrupulously in the wild prairie, knowing full well that it would not survive. Sobbing in his voice, he questioned his future. He wa so weak and defenseless, what was to become of him ?

Touched by his distress, Little Daisy was moved. She offered to stay with her, he would no longer be alone and would have enough to eat. Was she not a born huntress ?

He accepted at once. The girl increased her pace forward before the gnome could speak more. His manner of speaking made her uncomfortable. She tended, as much as possible, to reduce her time of words. A head smaller than her, Eye of Toad also had shorter legs. He had to trot to follow her rhythm, which prevented him from speaking.

Once at the river, she sent the gnome to pick up dead branches. During this interlude, she grabbed a carp the length of her arm. After a close battle, she hoisted it on the bank. Eye of Toad was ecstatic about this catch. The tongue hanging, he almost drooled. Twenty minutes later, both of them enjoyed a good peace of grilled fish, tender at will. Tubers and berries complemented this delicious meal.

Evening was falling. Already the sky was darkening and picking up sparkling points. With his mouth full, Eye of Toad questioned.

- And you, Little Daisy, besides your name, you did not tell me about you. What are you doing in the midst of this hostile prairie ? Would you have gone astray ?

She shook her head. The reflection of the fire played on his luminous skin.

- The prairie is not hostile to those who understand it. I'm not strayed away either.

- Not lost ?

Little Daisy had no reason to conceal the purpose of her expedition. Was not Eye of Toad even more distraught than she? And would it not be a travelling companion for the days to come ? He had the right to know where they would head.

- I'm doing a mission. I go to the West Mountains to pick up the Sun Stone and bring it home.

A spark lit in the perfidious gaze of the gnome. He dasked for more explanations. She willingly supplied them, without noticing the morbid gleam that danced in her companion's eyes as she spoke.

To the utterance of Black Sout, the wicked wizard, a terrible burst of light distorted the face of Eye of Toad. The gnome recovered very quickly. He formed an affable expression before Little Daisy could realized it.

In any case, she did not observe him. She remembered the frozen bodies of her tribe, men, women and children assembled in the village square. She was dreaming, melancholy, in front of the brands of the fire that blushed and cracked intermittently.

The conversation languished. Eye of Toad crookedly peered at the silent girl. Her face as pure as that of the moon, she was as innocent as the dew of the morning. Innocent and ... confident. At this thought, a mockery of smile twisted the face of the gnome. He caught the last piece of fish on the spit to plant his yellow and dirty teeth.

Little Daisy broke the silence.

"It is time to go to bed," she said, rising, "and tomorrow a long march awaits us."

She wrapped herself in her blanket, after having invited Eye of Toad to make a litter with the the supple grasses which grew in profusion around them. The gnome grumbled indistinct words but executed. Shortly afterwards, sleep spread its veil over this part of the bank.

CHAPTER 03

CAPTIVE

Usually the senses of Little Daisy were extremely sharp. However, the intensive walking in full sun, for days, had blunted them.

If her ear caught a commotion in the middle of the night, she did not record it or carry it to consciousness. It was only when a brutal clasp trapped her arms that she emerged from her sleep.

Half awake, she scarcely believed the picture that sister Moon was lighting up.

The gnome's head grimaced frightfully above her. More than ever, he deserved his name of Eye of Toad. She wanted to get up and found herself incapable of the slightest movement. She was tied up with her own rope. She shook herself, struggled, nothing was done. The more she struggled, the closer the ties were, and the more the gnome hooted at her with a squeaking laughter.

- Struggle as much as you like, Little Daisy, it will be a waste. You can believe me, I know in knots. You're not the first person that I tie up.

Upon this, he returned in a new neighing of evil joy. Little Daisy reared up savagely.

- Dirty betrayer ! Viper's tongue ! You are an insult to the living world.

The gnome sniggered dryly. He kicked the body lying on the ground. Quick, Little Daisy twisted abruptly and tried to bite his tibia. He stepped back a step.

- Little Daisy is lively, she needs exercises. If she reassures herself, they will soon !

He put on the little girl's bag and seized her arms. With a mocking smile, he passed the necklace of mother-of-pearl around his neck. The pearls tinkled against the large locket that was already dangling on his chest.

- Pretty, very pretty, he said, turning the necklace between his fingers. I know the value of the jewels, each of these pearls is worth a fortune. It is the assured wealth for my old age.

- My necklace, you dirty little thief !

- The compliments will be for later. For the moment, a long march is waiting for us.

The hunting knife of Little Daisy in his hand, he approached the little girl. She retreated. Eye of Toad cut off the bonds of his legs to the knees and quickly backed away. The bow of little Inikawas tensed as he pointed an arrow at her.

- Stand up, right now ! He ordered sharply. And do not imagine that I do not know how to use this weapon. I'm good archer. I never miss my target.

She began to get up. The operation was difficult, his bonds prevented her from moving properly. She succeeded, however.

- Go south ! I follow you. Do not try to run away, you would not go far.

The recommendation was useless, Little Daisy

had just the freedom necessary to accomplish a half-step. Rage in the heart, she found herself forced to progress according to the will of the gnome.

His sense of direction did not improved since the day before. Several times, he stopped to think and then change his way. They had been walking for several hours when the horizon finally turned pale. It took an hour more before the gnome was certain of him. At the exclamation he uttered, Little Daisy knew that they were coming to their destination.

She was not mistaken. A grove of scanty shrubs soon appeared in a gap. A horse was held at one of the trees by his halter. Near him stood a small country teepee of the size of a child. Undoubtedly, it belonged to the gnome.

Eye of Toad erupted a sigh of satisfaction.

- We have arrived at my camp. Frankly, I'm glad to see him again.

- You should never have left him, replied Little Daisy in an acid tone. I would have done without your company, it is odious to me.

Neglecting these last words, he resumed.

- Do you know that we could never have met ? Chance meant that the canary I held in captivity was released to perch on a stalk of these great grasses. I tried to catch it. Just when my hand was about to grab it, it flew away on another stem. Again, I rushed to him and the game began again. For half an hour I zigzagged from right to left until I reached the river. Your things dragged on the shore without anyone to keep them. The pearl necklace jumped at me. You were armed and I was not. I preferred to avoid a confrontation. Fortunately for me, your back was turned. I was able to serve myself without being noticed. I also picked up your boots to thwart your pursuit. Clever, is not it ?

Little Daisy did not flinch. Her gaze became hostile, the moment would come when the gnome would pay his crime ! Eye of Toad twisted his face into a grimace that was meant to be joyous.

- Yeah ! After all, it was not that clever because you ended up catching me. Without my horse and the height he gave me, I no longer had any landmarks. I lost a lot of time in the tall grass trying to find my nag

With a great gesture of his hand, he swept the space, looking pleased.

- Bah ! What matters is that everything ends well. The necklace is in my possession, what more can I ask ?

At the entrance of the grove, he tied Little Daisy to a tree, time for him to bend his tent and place it on his horse. He took a new rope, tied it around the girl's wrists, and fixed the other end to the saddle.

He then released the top of her leg and cut the tie of the tree. While doing that, he was still threatening Little Daisy with his tapered blade. It was unwelcome for her to try anything, especially since her hands were welded and her aggressor was on his guard at a distance.

The globular eye of the gnome discovered with satisfaction the contained rage of his prisoner. He moved back two steps and then jumped on his mount.

- As you said last night, Little Daisy, a long march awaits us today. It will be certainly more trying than you imagined. Let's go !

The horse started suddenly. The shock surprised the little Inikawas. She staggered, but caught herself at the last moment.

The gnome sneered. It would not have displeased him to see her fall. The horse advanced at a pace. Despite this, he went faster than Little Daisy. So she was forced to trot behind him so as not to be dragged on the ground like a vulgar pack of dirty linen. The gnome turned round several times to see her. He cheerily commented on the stumbles of the one he "protected" as he said.

Boiling with rage, she retorted.

- I have nothing to do with your protection, set me free ! I have no use for you.

- Hm, hm !

- You have my necklace, you have recognized yourself it worth a fortune. I offer it to you in exchange for my freedom.

- How can you offer something that is no longer yours ? He argued unctuously, tapping the pearls. It is mine, now you no longer possess anything.

- Since I possess nothing, I can only clutter you. Break Me !

- And for what reason ?

- You know, I'm on a mission. I go to the setting sun to look for the Sun Stone. This crystal is more precious to me than all the pearls and jewels of the world. I give you everything, necklace, weapon, bag. I just ask you to let me accomplish my mission and save my tribe, the Inikawas.

He turned abruptly toward her and let go.

- Because you did not yet understand ?

Trotting behind the horse, Little Daisy was surprised at the question.

- Understood, what ?

This question filled with joy Eye of Toad.

He uttered two or three neighs typical of his good mood. He then deigned to explain.

- It was precisely to prevent you from reaching the Sun Stone that I captured you.

- What ! But, then, you are ... you would be ...

- Black Soot ? No, alas no ! I do not have his powers either. I am but one of his humble and faithful servants.

Dismayed, Little Daisy came to a halt, her mouth open. She took it badly. The horse had not slowed down. She was ejected forward. It was as if somebody were pulling out her arms. The pain in her shoulders was terrible, yet she repressed a cry of suffering. She would not concede any complaint, not even a groan to the minion of Black Soot. Eye of Toad went on, swaggering.

- The Inikawas received only the legitimate punishment of their obstinacy. They have refused submission to a master-sorcerer who exceeds them a thousand times, it is only fair that they have been petrified. The chance wanted you to be out of the way at that very moment, which saved you from mummification. However, instead of being discreet and hiding in a hole, you had the ambition to break the fate of Black Soot. It is a sacrilegious act ! Do you know that I was present during the rigidification of your tribe ? It was great art, work done nicely ! My master will be very happy to learn more about the last words of your grandmother and to have an additional slave in her service. Perhaps he will even give me your hand as a reward.

- What ! You would not have the audacity ...?

- When one carries out such an interesting capture, one can afford all daring. It will be up to my master to hear me.

- Never, you hear me, never ! Rather die !

He launched a long stridulation synonymous with the most intense joy. Little Daisy was horrified. Anger gave her a red mask on his face. The wildest rage rumbled in her soul. In despair, she bit the thick rope tied around her wrists, determined to gnaw at it until the last fiber.

The torrid sun burned her cheeks and her throat. She had not drunk anything since the day before. By sadism, Eye of Toad swallowed the water of her gourd so loudly as to stir up her prisoner's thirst. He ostensibly crunched the fruit and chewed the dried meat so preciously preserved by the little Inikawas.

Little Daisy was silent. His teeth bite the rope. Fibers had already broken, but it was still far from being released. The task she had set herself was almost impossible in the conditions in which she found herself. The horse pulled her and her own irregular trot hindered the movements of her jaws.

However, she persisted. She struggled for her freedom, for the freedom of her own.

His ear was permanently assaulted by the bragging Eye of Toad. He explained in detail how his master had taken it to defeat this tribe less than anything the Inikawas were. He added for himself a favorable role in the accomplishment of this victory, a totally invented role as Little Daisy assumed. Black Soot did not need a gnome to cast a spell. His own evil powers were enough. However, Eye of Toad boasted of several glorious actions. After a few hours, he had said so much, that one would have thought that without his help, Black Soot would never have overcome the Inikawas. If he did not go so far as to pretend to have petrified the village with his own hand, somebody could imagine that.

This idle babbling had at least the advantage of providing Little Daisy with valuable information about his enemy and learning that the wizard's lair was two days' walk away. After leaving the lifeless village of the Inikawas, the sorcerer galloped toward another unfortunate tribe to subdue. This time, Eye of Toad was not with him. His master had sent him to prepare a reception worthy of him, in view of his next return. Eye of Toad had been caught capturing canaries. Black Soot loved to pluck the feathers from them one by one. It was thus that the gnome fell on the last of the Inikawas.

While the gnome was congratulating himself on his good fortune, Little Daisy listened with an attentive ear, continuing to gnaw at his bonds. The hard fibers cracked one after another under his teeth.

The afternoon was already well under way when she finally felt the rope relax. She bit even harder. Eye of Toad was not aware of anything. He heard the trampling of his captive behind him and that was enough for him. For the rest, he did not care much about it. The more exhausted she would be, the less likely she would be to cause trouble.

- Tomorrow evening we shall have arrived, he replied once more. You will have the privilege of submit to Black Soot, the face against the ground. Perhaps he will allow you to lift your gaze on his person, but it is not sure. A slave must always keep his eyes lowered.

His speech suddenly choked. Little Daisy had just lifted him by one leg and tipped him over the other side of the horse. An exclamation of pain and a growl followed the fall of Eye De Toad in the grass.

He got up very quickly, with the knife in front, panicked by the turn of events. Like a flash, Little Daisy threw herself on the gnome. He had no time to knock, she had imprisoned his wrist in a steely gip. At the same time, she threw her knee in his stomach. He folded down a horrible yell. His hand released the knife.

Little Daisy compressed her fingers. All the anger accumulated since her capture was transmitted into his arm. Her fist hit the gnome on the chin as he was raising and sent him back tumbled down. She grabbed the weapon and turned to him.

He lay in freshly crushed grass. Even closed, his globular eyes had lost nothing of their hideousness. She stepped cautiously, perhaps he was pretending to be unconscious. No, he was out of action ! Stunned, not dead as his immobility could have made her think.

“ The evil birds of his kind have life pegged to their putrid soul ! She declared sententiously."

She hesitated a few seconds before making a decision. The, with a rapid movement, she detached the rope from the saddle of the horse and tied the gnome. " The good fellow will have a real surprise when he awakes, " she thought happily, " he will have had only what he deserves! "

Noticeing a shrub not far from there, she dragged the inanimate gnome and tied him firmly.

CHAPTER 04

The jailer prisoner

Eye of Toad was slow to find his way. Little Daisy repressed a pout of disgust. His aggressor, unable to defend himself against a girl, was just good at stealing them and bind them during their sleep.

Having run so long, she was exhausted, but resisted, however, to the dejection of her muscles. However, before she left, she had to eat and rest. His body, thirsty, howled. She forced herself to drink in sips and at regular intervals. Too much water after all these hours to burn in the sun would have made her sick. By munching away small pieces of meat, she swallowed from time to time a sip of her leather flask.

She had almost finished eating when the gnome manifested itself by a series of groans. Little Daisy approached him.

- Here you are, revived, nasty snake ! You are not even worth the rope that serves as your bonds.

The gnome opened his eyes full of total incomprehension. He still did not really realize his position. An harsh sentence of Little Daisy tore the mists of his mind.

- I was waiting for you to be awake to watch my departure.

He stuttered with astonishment.

- Your departure ?

- Hon, hon !And before, I will recover what is mine.

She took off her necklace of pearls from the neck of Eye of Toad to pass it around hers.

- A gift from my grandmother, I still could not leave it to you ! Moreover, for having forced me to run behind your horse all day, you owe me reparation.

The gnome cried out.

- Do not protest so much ! You did not hesitate to rob me and to inflict on me the suffering of thirst and race. Count yourself happy that I do not want your life. I shall only take you a little trifle, but that will go very well on me.

With a sharp gesture, she appropriated his golden medallion and placed it around her neck as well. The reaction of Eye of Toad was disproportionate with regard to the value of the jewel. He ceased his outraged roars when Little Daisy asked him to choose between the medallion or his life in return for what she had endured for a dozen hours.

He remained silent for a moment, then, seeing her turn back, inquired anxiously.

- What are you going to do with me now ? To attach myself to my horse to take me to your suite as far as the West Moutains ? I do not walk as fast as you, I'll only delay you. So do not you clutter at me.

- That was my intention ! I will not bother with your perfidious tongue. I no longer wish to see you again in all my existence.

He seemed relieved of great weight. Already, colors were returning to his dismal face.

- I knew you were not a bad girl. As soon as you have liberated me, I will go to my side. I promise not to cause you any trouble anymore. I'll gallop without turning around.

- No !

- How, no ?

- I'm taking the horse.

- But you never rode in your life ! The Inikawas are ignorant of the use of horses. You do not have any in your village.

- Undeceive yourself ! We used to have one. He died of old age this winter. Like the other children of the tribe, I learned to direct it. I keep yours for compensation.

- You already have my pendant !

- Then consider that it is a compensation for

what your master has done to mine. He will give you another one. Let's see this one !

She jumped on the saddle and pushed her hair back. She amused herself in advancing the horse, in making it turn and turn. When she was certain she had it, she exclaimed.

- He's very sweet ! I think we'll make a good team ... Come on, bye Eye of Toad ! You will wish a bad day on my part to Black Soot. May his misdeeds torment him every night !

- Hey ! Little Daisy ?

- What now ? You do not want me to thank your master for the fate he has thrown on mine.

- It's not that. You just forgot to untie me.

The smile of Little Daisy blossomed.

- To untie you ?

- Yes, to untie me.

- But I do not intend it at all.

Mouth open, the gnome thought for a second that she wanted to tickle him, teasing him by the simple spirit of revenge. The resolution he read in his gestures and expression dissipated his misunderstanding.

- You can not do that to me, Little Daisy, not you ! To leave me bound to this tree is to send me to death. I shall die of hunger and thirst, devoured by ants and rats. Little Daisy, you so sweet, so kind, you can not inflict such a torture on a weak defenseless creature.

- Your wailing no longer works, Eye of Toad ! You duped me once, I understood the lesson ! I said that you will stay tied up, I'll not go back on that. To rescue you, you have only to imitatewhat I did. Gnaw the rope !

At these words, the gnome shouted out new wounds. He begged her to throw a dagger at his feet so that he could cut off his bonds himself. He appealed to his heart, to the solidarity of men. She remained inflexible. He complained of his teeth, of the weakness of his jaws. He would never be able to gnaw at his rope.

Little Daisy decided she had heard enough.

- That's enough, Eye of Toad ! I know you now, and I know the perfidy of your tongue. Your words are only lies. Know that I am not fool. Know also that I do not impose this trial on you by a spirit of revenge or pleasure. Prudence would have me to stick an arrow in your heart. But I do not want to shoot down a human creature, no matter how miserable, especially when he is incapable of defending himself. I leave life to you, but I shall not let you run to your master to seek reinforcements. You would do that, I guess. So I want to keep enough time for me to leave. The time you will take to the end of your bonds will allow me to move away and be safe. When you come to Black Soot, I will be out of reach.

The Gnome gave her a hateful look. The evil reigning in his heart then appeared on his heavy features, without a mask. He heaped abuse on her, tons of insults, shout to her the worst curses.

Little Daisy welcomed them with a crystalline

laugh which annihilated them. She slightly slapped on the horse's flank with her foot. He reared before galloping, heading towards the west. The laugh of little Inikawas resounded on the spot long after she had disappeared.

The horse leaped through the great meadow. Like an arrow, he made his way to the lair of the sun. The long hair of Little Daisy flew in its wake. The wind whipped her face. She shouted with joy, greedy of speed. His mount seemed tireless. After having dawdle during the day when the little girl wa swalking, it could not stop running.

They continued thus for nearly an hour. The little Inikawas was so full with happiness ! From her high position, she overlooked the tall grass and moved faster than she had ever done. It was an amazing sensation. For nothing in the world, she would have wanted her ride to stop.

As a wise huntress, she thought of her mission. At this speed, she would exhaust her horse in half an hour. She therefore reduced it to an reasonable gallop, perfectly attuned to the possibilities of the animal.

As she approached the night, she discovered a pool of clear water from the top of her saddle. Nothing could be easier, the surface of the water formed a mirror in the middle of the green land. She made a halt there, time to water her horse, to quench hers' thirst and to dig tubers. The gnome had been voracious. Her bag was empty but she did not want to linger hunt.

The wizard's den was a day's walk from where she had attached the gnome, that meant a few hours from where she was. In this case, a Black Soot patrol had the opportunity to join her and capture her. She had not yet won, far from it !

When her mount was refreshed, she sat back in the saddle.

Riding at night was dangerous, darkness could hide unforeseen obstacles, but the rising moon dispelled the fears of Little Daisy. Its silver light illuminated enough the meadow to allow a rider to progress without difficulty.

An owl hooted. It was frightened when it heard the sustained gallop which disturbed him in his watch. Foxes barked. Nor were they used to the nocturnal rides. The higher mammals of their territory - antelopes or bison - only moved by day. Many other little animals raised an alarmed ear to listen to this suspicious anomaly. No catastrophe occurred, and the echo of the hoofs was lost in the distance; they relaxed their vigilance and returned to their occupations.

For hours, Little Daisy pushed her horse. In the midst of the night, exhausted by her long and exhausting vigil, aching and stiff everywhere, she stopped her mount. The halter of the horse quickly wrapped around a bunch of solid bamboos, she let him graze as he pleased and sank into his blanket. Sleep fell upon her as soon as her eyelids stooped.

At the same moment, Eye of Toad had broken his bonds. His heart full of gall, he had act according to the indications of his former captive. Although yellow, and despite his protests, his canines teeth were sturdy. He chewed for hours on the rope which enclosed him, the saliva poured on his chin and his cheeks mixed with vegetable crumb.

When the last fiber broke under his molars, he rejected his ties with rage. His globular eyes were burning with vengeance. The hooting of an owl triggered in his body a shudder of fright. He realized suddenly that he was alone and disarmed in a land open to the wind. The ideal prey of a predator !

Panic seizes him. He began to run.

The brownish trunk of a rickety beech tree appeared before him. The tree was not very high, but it appeared to the gnome scared as a fortress amid innumerable enemies.

Until morning, he remained hanging on the fork of a master branch, shivering with anguish. He groaned at each creaking and cracking. The hissing of the wind seemed to hide the crawling of wild beasts. His own snaps of teeth made him nervous.

The rays of dawn found him hugging the trunk of the beech, as he was beset to indescribable terror. With daybreak, resentment took over his fear. He jumped at the foot of the tree, and trotted towards his village, determined to make Little Daisy pay the night of terror he had passed.

CHAPTER 05

In the wizard's den.

The thoughts of Little Daisy were very far from the horrible little gnome. At the moment when Eye of Toad was finally deciding to dismount, she had been galloping for almost an hour already. His brief hours of sleep had dissipated his tiredness.

When she awoke, she only took the time to drink two sips to her gourd, pick an harmful of red and black berries and make sure of the condition of her mount. It was dashing and only wanted exercise. Laughing, little Inikawas jumped on her back and then started.

Like the day before, the ride was a bit of a laugh. She was amused to see her long brown hair float behind her. His joyful laughter often broke out during his ride. His back hurt, but an Inikawas despised the pain. She overcome it and then concentrated on the wind that caressed her face.

Sometimes, the rays of the sun snatched flashes of lightning from the medallion. He swayed on his chest to the rhythm of the gallop. The left hand holding the horse's bridle, she lifted it with her right hand. It was oddly crafted, consisting of a multitude of geometric patterns welded in a precise order. What could they mean ?

Puzzled, Little Daisy released him. It was of no use to wear out the thought about an enigma of which she could not get the answer. Her sharp spirit was again carried away by the excitement of the ride. She forgot all that was not herself, the horse and the ocean of grass that was waving.

The halts were brief and rare, not for her but for her mount. She wanted to keep it fresh and in excellent shape. So she stopped from time to time to give him something to drink.

For that, she curved her left hand, filled it with

water and handed it to the hose. It was quick to aspire the meager content. She repeated the operation several times before getting back into the saddle. She, on the other hand, only allowed herself somme drops. The capacity of her leather flask was limited - ten liters in all of which there were only three left. Her mount which provided the painful work of progression passed before her.

The height of her position enlarged her horizon. At dusk, a long silvery snake meandered far in front of her. Little Daisy shudders with joy. Shortly afterwards, she threw herself on her stomach over a singing stream. The icy water had an incomparable flavor.

The horse imitated him. He greedily grew this fruit of life by plunging his nostrils. He then shook them with loud neighing. His mistress let him nibble on the tender grass of the bank to look for his own subsistence. A plump hare started to run ten meters away. She made a brief apology for him, while shooting it with a quick arrow. A rabbit finishes the same way.

An hour later, she thanked both of them for the gift of their flesh by watching them roast with the burning flame of a wood fire. She ate only part of the hare, accompanied by tubers and berries. The rabbit and the rest of the hare were wrapped in large leaves.

These provisions were too precious to allow them to vanish in one meal. The country she passed through was foreign to her. She did not know if the next days she would find the game necessary for her survival, such precautions were therefore imperative. Before going to bed, she inspected the brook upstream. A shrub, short and broad, furnishes her with large yellow fruits in abundance. She hastened to bring back as much as she could.

Her supplies ready for several days, Little Daisy said how pleased she was. A smile of contentment flourished on her fine face before she slipped into a deep sleep.

As the final crescent of the moon set its first rays on the dark hair of the little Inikawas, a few miles away, its lit up a strange scene.

At the entrance of a monumental mound in the shape of a truncated pyramid, two griffins - creatures with lion's body and eagle's head - stretched their impressive claws towards a caricature of a man. Their beaks shone in the half-darkness.

- You do not have your symbol of recognition, Eye of Toad, one of them growled. You are therefore only an intruder.

- And every intruder who crosses this line, adds the second, pointing to an imaginary point, is considered a game. Your small size will only appreciate the flavor of your flesh.

The tempest gnome threatened the two griffins of Black Soot's anger but did not advance. The two warders of the wizard's den were ordered to forbid the entry to anyone who did not possess the official pass, a specially forged pendant that the master of the place temporarily entrusted to one of its principal henchmen during a mission.

Eye of Toad cursed the little Inikawas.

Without knowing it, she had deprived him of all means of penetrating into the mound. From then on, he could not trigger the alert and undertake a beat to find her before the return of Black Soot. None of the servants would respond to his calls, no one ventured outside in the sorcerer's absence. The griffins were not pernickety about the quality of their game. They devoured all those who did not wear the pendant or were not led by the bearer of a pendant, and none of the inhabitants had any.

He showered these fierce guards with abuses and insults, knowing that their chains allowed them only a five-meter displacement around the door. Conscious of their constraint, the griffins merely looked at him of their big wild eyes, always eager for fresh flesh. Their split pupils reflected no doubt about their intentions if he tried to penetrate their range of action.

Eye of Toad thought it prudent to move back. From afar, he shouted invectives over the two sentries. He burst to them with the most insulting names, blasted the memory of their fathers and the fathers of their fathers, and then, finding himself short of ideas, went down to a half-ruined hut.

Black Soot would not be back for two days. So he'll have to live all this time in this slum. However, the worst was not the disgusting floor where he would spend the night, nor the spoiled food he saw himself forced to swallow, but the fury of his master.

When the sorcerer returned from his campaigns and noticed that no great entertainments would receive him according to his orders, he would directly attack him. Eye of Toad knew him well enough to know him cruel and quick to punish.

The two days that followed, he lived in a real agony. The two griffins were always present. When one of them disappeared in the mound to shred some bloody prey, the second encreased its watchful. On the first day he went up to see them several times. The hungry gaze which the wild beasts darted upon his person quickly removed all attraction from these visits. He ended by no longer leaving his wretched shelter. In one corner of the hut he found food not too mouldy. He devoured this infamous food with grimaces and squeals.

On the evening of the second day a heavy silence fell on the mound and on the surrounding lands. Even the air was heavy; He crushed the neighborhood.

A trampling soon torn the thick atmosphere. Bellowing, squawking and giggling followed shortly. Eye of Toad rushed out.

Many deformed creatures, half-men, half-animals, climbed the path leading to the mound.

In the midst of them, on a gigantic black horse, came a tall horseman. A black cape enveloped his bony body, a hood covered his head. Falling over his eyes, it forbade an attentive examination of his expression. However, one could guess at the harshness of the features of the chin and the cheekbones, a cruel character.

A mist seemed constantly floating on the face of the man, veiling his skin nevertheless white.

The darkness of his soul imprinted itself on his face.

Convulsive tremors shook Eye of Toad. He threw himself at the foot of the black horse. It was disgusting to see such terror and servility.

- Oh ! My master, Black Soot. Forgive your wretched slave for not being able to execute all your orders.

On a gesture of the sorcerer, the troop stopped. The conversations, odious gurgle rumbles and onomatopoeia, ceased immediately. A husky voice, full of threats, thundered.

- What is it, son of a bitch ? Tell me how is it that no reception receives me with the honors due to me ? Would you have the presumption to brave my orders ?

A horrible groan went out from the throat of the

gnome. He plunged his head again into the dust. Sprawled on the ground with his arms stretching in front, he appealed to his master's clemency. The air was charged with electricity. Black Soot barked.

- Speak up ! Explain what happens otherwise my griffins will feed on your feeble body !

The words whipped Eye of Toad.

"Pity, master ! I am only your slave. All this is the fault of a perverse child whom the fate has thrown me between my legs.

The gnome unloaded his misadventure, insisting on the deceitfulness of his former captive. As the wave of his rancor poured down, the sorcerer's features darkened.

A latent hatred of incredible strength blackened his face.

His eyes, clear at the beginning, were only two pieces of rotten coal. The seemingly calm words he uttered perspired the cruelty.

- How did you tell me she is called ?

- Little Daisy, my master, the last of the

Inikawas. She may have only twelve springs, but she is no longer a little girl. She stole the pendant, preventing me from entering the mound and preparing your welcome. We must punish her severely for this unqualified crime, oh, my lord !

Black De Suie exploded. The violence of his words shook the griffins at the entrance.

- What ! The talisman I told you !

Eye De Toad wiggled in the dust moaning.

- By the curse of the viper, how could you allow such a misdeed to perpetrate ? This pendant is not a simple jewel. If ever she discovers its power and the way to use it ...

He did not finish his sentence, but everyone, from the smallest homunculus to the griffins, felt that the danger would be terrible. At a sign from the wizard, creatures of the troop seized Eye of Toad and then all entered into the mound.

The pyramid was vast, and a whole village was lodged there. Black Soot had it built by the numerous slaves taken from the neighboring tribes, like the pyramids existing in the island-continent of Atlantis. When he had enslaved the whole country, he would bring up others more imposing, even if he had to dry up the region of its inhabitants.

In the center of the pyramid, a large hall served as both a temple and a residence for the master of the place. Semi-human creatures jostled to open the doors and prepare the litter that served as his seat.

Without taking notice of the paws he was crushing in his progress, Black Soot stepped forward. He sat down cross-legged. Two of his servants, akin to pigs, installed cushions to support his back. He pushed them away and concentrated on the scene in front of him. According to his orders, the gnome was tied to a beam by the wrists.

Eye of Toad moaned pitifully. His entreaties increased when his tunic was snatched from him. His greasy torso appeared to be blistered as he was stuffed. Near him, a creature like a badly shaped cock rode on a man's body played with a whip, looking happy.

- Master, I beg you ! Do not hurt your slave ! Master, have I not faithfully executed your orders to this day ? Have I not, to please you, roast a dozen men at the last reception ?

- You did it, Eye of Toad, you did it ! But where is the reception today ?

- I was planning a raid on a family I had spotted during my return. But the little Inikawas deceived me. By stealing my horse and the pendant, she prevented me from entering the mound and taking with me a troop to capture these primitives and organize the entertainment I intended for you. You must chastise her, oh my master !

- It will be done, I assure you, my good Eye of Toad. However, this expedition among the wild tribes has wearied me. I need some distractions. This is your job and the reason I gave you my trust and my talisman. You have failed, so I must improvise. Tonight you will have the honor of being the star of my evening.

He raised his arms and clamoured.

- Let the rejoicings begin !

At the end of the hall, homunculus beat on tambourines. The whip fell in cadence. Every time it lashed the gnome's shoulders, a murmur of joy rose from the monstrous audience. The screams of Eye of Toad resounded under the vault to the public's delight.

Certainly the spectacle was not as spicy as what they were used to, but to see the favorite of the sorcerer screaming with grief delighted them. The gnome had always been haughty towards them. He had taken advantage of his position to inflict a thousand torments on them.

Seeing him thus forced into execution was a great joy.

When the gnome fainted and the audience could not take any pleasure from its suffering, Black Soot stopped the executioner.

Eye of Toad was removed and left on the ground.

CHAPTER 06

An odious attack

Later, after Black Soot and his troop had filled their hunger and thirst, the sorcerer revived the gnome. Eye of Toad was already conscious for a long time, but, fearing a new need for entertainment from his master, he had prudently opted for immobility. Well-placed kicks quickly put him on foot.

- Approach ! Ordered the sorcerer, and tell me about this girl !

Eye of Toad related everything he knew about the little Inikawas, that is to say, very few. Wanting to divert the rage from Black Soot, he suggested.

- Why do not you strike this impudent little person, at a distance, as I have seen you do on several occasions ? Your black magic can burn her.

- She could if that plague did not wear the talisman. Did not I tell you that it was magical ? It was forged in the old Atlantis according to a precise rite. The charm he unfolded would repel my mystical fluid.

- So she's invincible ?

A frightening gleam oscillated in the darkness of the sorcerer's eyes.

- Invincible ? No, surely not ! She is protected from mystical attacks, not from a physical blow, whether it comes from a man or an animal. She is vulnerable to the tooth of a wild beast or the arrow of a hunter. And the meadow has more traps than she imagines.

He stood up quickly. The tail of a monkey-like creature crashed under his foot, snatching yellings from its owner. Giggles rose beyond. The troops never missed an opportunity to rejoice.

- We must stop this girl, not merely for revenge, for having appropriated a good belonging to me.

This is a minor point. No, the reason is more important. She goes to fetch the Sun Stone. I had heard of this crystal without knowing where it was. Now I know its location, the West Mountains. May she manage to win her village and the Inikawas will be delivered from my spell. Their dean, that very old woman came from Atlantis, is fine enough to guess the use of the talisman. Hence it is only a step to make use of it against me, and join the tribes of the country with it. She is capable of crossing it. That would be the end of my domination !

He turned abruptly toward the gnome and grabbed him by the throat.

- Do you now understand the scope of your actions ? Do you understand the reason of this fury which devours me ?

The sorcerer's grip strangled the gnome. It could only emit incomprehensible borborygms. When he was on the brink of asphyxia, Black Soot released him. Eye of Toad fell on the ground, his body flabby, his tongue hanging down, breathing with difficulties.

Without further concern, the sorcerer advanced towards the back of the room. A large plate covered with a thick woolen fabric was held vertically on a pedestal. With a quick movement of his wrist he removed the fabric. A black crystal the size of a man and a perfect oval appeared to the audience. Silence suddenly fell. Everyone knew the function of this monolith. They feared and venerated him, but for nothing in the world would have liked to approach it.

- The talisman is connected to the pyramid by a magic bond, it is a chance for us ! We will locate it easily.

Facing the monolith, the sorcerer threw his head back. The black hood covered his face a little more, so that no one could guess his expression. A lugubrious song raised up from the bottom of his throat, a horrible chant that made the most experienced ones shudder.

The crystal cleared as he sang. When he had finished, on its polished side, a landscape appeared as clearly as if it really existed in the room. In the dark blue sky, the moon was practically complete. He bathed a clearing in his silver light. In the background flowed a stream, a thin black iridescent ribbon in the darkness. The half-human creatures caught all that at a glance, but their attention was fixed on the white horse attached to a tree, on the half-extinguished fireplace and above all, on the small form lying in the grass .

Wrapped in a blanket, nothing could be distinguished except a very brown hair and a face whose whiteness and purity rivaled those of the moon.

- Little Daisy ! Belched the gnome.

On his knees beside his master, he opened his eyes even more monstrous than usual.

- It is her, I recognize her ! It was her who stole the medallion.

- I see ! Replied Black Soot.

- How can she sleep as serenely and without the protection of a tepee, when the prairie buzzes with dangers ? I have experienced such an experience and am not ready to start again.

- Innocence and purity protect as much as a talisman, it is known !

To this evidence, Eye of Toad made no reply. The wizard also remained pensive for a moment before his hand tensed violently.

- I hate innocence and purity. They have always been obstacles to my ambitions. I will not allow this continent to be renewed. If only for this reason, this girl must die !

He glanced at the mirror.

- Let us ensure that his sleep is eternal !

Brief and precise orders were heard in the hall. Shortly afterwards, a wailing kid goat vas brought and also an obsidian dagger on a silver platter. The kid goat was laid down and tied to a black granite slab at the base of the monolith. Black Soot immediately undertook a ritual of sorcery. He chanted an odious litany to hear. Some of the assistants plugged their ears so much that the bellowing exceeded the unnameable.

The heart in serenity, Little Daisy slept peacefully, rocked by the warm breeze. A burn tickled her chest briefly. She moved slightly and wanted to return to her dreams. She was again at the gates of this marvelous world that opened to her at night when unusual rustlings puzzled her. The wind, no doubt, she said to herself in her half-sleep. Soon these noises turned into slips and furtive squeals.

Little Daisy jumped immediately on his feet. Her ear had just recognized them, and his whole being was shouting " Danger ! ".

The horse also understood. He neighs with fear. At the moment when Little Daisy was throwing his blanket on the back of his mount, Black Soot sacrificed the kid goat. At that very moment a red-hot iron burned the little girl's chest, whilst the rustlings filled the night so much that it seemed like the buzz of a hive.

Little Inikawas lost no time in asking questions, she tied her bag on the horse. Her bow was on the other side of the hearth, she could not leave without him. As she darted, whistles froze her. Two serpents stood before her, ready to bite. In a fraction of a second, her tomahawk was in his hand and both heads cut. In the same movement, she leaped over the hearth, picked up her bow and ... the horror twitched in her eyes.

Beyond the clearing, and over tens of meters, the meadow was covered with snakes.

Many were unknown to her, but all she identified was mortal. No more question of jumping on horseback and running away. The moving carpet, which moved as a wave, would have bitten its mount a thousand times before it could cross it. The poor beast would be instantly overwhelmed by the dazzling venom and she, Little Daisy, submerged in the following seconds.

A quick glance offered her the vision of tens of thousands of serpents waving treacherously from all directions. The clearing was surrounded. They would soon be on it !

The instinct of conservation burst forth a fabulous energy in her hearts. Whatever the number of her adversaries, she would fight. An Inikawas never surrendered !

She grabbed a glowing brand. Faced with an enemy with thousands of heads and fangs, slippery bodies, there was only a parry: the fire !

Little Daisy acted quickly. Her goal was to create a circle of fire to drive back the snakes. The first grasses touched by the burning wood ignited timidly. The little fire she had managed to light on both sides were very meager to stop her adversaries. Already a number had entered the clearing. Each time she bent down to light a clump of grass, one, two, or three heads showed up, the bifid tongue pointing at her. Her reflexes narrowly saved her several times.

About thirty snakes lay, their heads cut off. But the others, thousands of others crowded, eager to plant their fangs in her thin arms

She was desperate. Why did not the fire take ? He was sometimes so quick to trigger of his own free will, why did it refuse it now, when she put all his will into it ? Yet the grass were dry. Little Daisy persisted. The brand in one hand, she went from one edge of the clearing to another, jumped aside to avoid a tongue, a pair of fangs, cutting a head here and there. Despite her efforts, the fire was limited. Small of them burned here and there, slowing down the advance of the snakes, too puny to stop them.

Then came the moment when she found herself wedged to her horse. The clearing rustled with snakes.

Suddenly a wall of flame rose up around. Little Daisy received the breath of the fire in the face. A smell of roasted flesh attacked her nostrils : snakes burned in hundreds. The others were fleeing. Even those present in the clearing neglected their prey to think only of saving their lives. Instinctive reaction, they went in common agreement to the only passage free of flames, that leading to the stream.

The fire roared in torrid waves. Little Daisy felt the danger. The fire would burn her on the spot if she did not also run away.

The retreat towards the brook was forbidden to her; It was swarme with snakes. The mind sharp, she studyed the situation and responded promptly. She had scarcely found a solution that her hand was ahead of her to go to her leather flask. The ten liters of water soaked the horse's legs, chest and head. She jumped on her mount. After moistening with the last lamps and then being wrapped tightly in her blanket, she threw her horse at full gallop.

The horse snorted for a moment, but, spurred on by his rider and dying of fear and the need to flee, he leaped through the flames. The panic created by the arrival of snakes and the appearance of the fire gave him wings.

He split the wall of fire so quickly that Little Daisy did not immediately realize that she was saved. She was choking, her nose under the blanket, while the smoke irritated her throat and fogged her eyes. When at last she could see clearly, the horse had taken the bit between its teeth. She could no longer control it. He was heading straight for the west.

CHAPTER 07

The buffaloes' rush

In the large room in the heart of the pyramid, Black Soot howled with fury. He seized the abandoned whip and knocked all those close to his hand. Desperate squeals rose from all sides. The deformed creatures asked for trembling grace from their grotesque members.

His anger calmed down, he returned to the mirror. Little Daisy was still running in a disheveled ride, unable to control his mount. The sorcerer grabbed the kid by one of his legs and sent it over the audience.

- Let some one bring me another! he exploded. It will not be said that a primitive girl will have held me up !

His servants not going fast enough according to his will, he flogged them.

- A goat immediately, or one of you will take it place !

Wailings of fright filled the room. Everyone rushed in search of the animal.

* * *

Tens of miles away, Little Daisy had many other worries. His horse was galloping for half an hour and it was impossible to control it. If at first she had been delighted that they were moving away from both the fire and the snakes, after a while, she was concerned. Her leather flak was was empty and she had lost her food. In her haste, she had hung them badly, they had untied and fall down at the first bounds.

Gradually, Little Daisy gave way to a slight somnolence. Her arms hugging the neck of her horse, she was trying to recover her strength and a little sleep this night shorted.

- Brother horse will eventually stop when he

gets tired, she thought. We go towards the west. It will be as much time in less for my expedition. "

A sudden change in the rhythm of the horse's run made her jump. She had fallen asleep without realizing it. With astonishment, she saw that the day was bright. The horse had run for hours.

From the top of her mount, she contemplated with delight the clear mass which was cut out in the blue of the sky. The West Mountains were there within reach. She could have touched the buttresses. However, she did not cradle any illusion. The mountain was not as close as it seemed. It would take another two days before reaching it.

By association of ideas she bent over her mount. It was on the verge of exhaustion, incapable of advancing otherwise than at a pace. His lungs rose and descended at an alarming rate. His breath resounded with shudder.

Little Daisy jumped into the grass. She picked up a large handful to groom the horse. She had no water to offer. She contented herself with speaking calmly and examining it. Its skin had scorched in various places, superficial burns. It speed combined with the water which she had prudently poured out of it, had annihilated the action of the flames. It needed only rest.

A too sudden immobility after a very long physical effort is always detrimental to health, Little Daisy knew it since she was old enough to shoe herself her boots. She drew her horse by the halter and walked towards the West Moutains in little steps.

This slow progress increased her concern. Her eyes only saw a dry grass, tall yellow stalks - the obvious sign of a lack of water. It had not rained in the area since moons and, given the state of the grass, streams were rare. The problem of water would soon come to her, especially under such a strong sun. With a leather flask full of water, Little Daisy had seen the future in a less gloomy light. Alas, that was not the case ! She no longer had a single drop.

Fruits could have contained his thirst and that of his horse, but the rickety trees were devoid of them.

Suddenly a huge break appeared in the midst of the prairie. The crushed grass plowed the vegetal ocean with a rectilinear feature over a hundred yards wide. Brownish mounds dotted this surprising alley.

- Buffaloes ! Exclaimed Little Daisy.

She repeated to the attention of her riding companion.

- Buffaloes have passed through here, Brother horse. A gigantic herd Have you noticed the trail they left behind them ?

She leaned over one of the mounds. A nauseating odour emanated from it, and for good reason it was the droppings of the animals. On examination, she deduced that they had traveled recently for less than an hour.

She informed her horse and, at the same time, Black Soot to whom the talisman allowed to see and hear what was happening in the immediate vicinity of the last Inikawas.

The sorcerer arrived just in time to catch those words. As long as the horse galloped, he could not do anything against Little Daisy. She was moving too fast for him to take any action. So he had to wait for the animal to get tired.

Through the hours, lassitude had won him. He had stretched himself on his bunk, not without having posted one of his servants in front of the mirror, with orders to wake him as soon as the beast had stopped.

The voice of Little Daisy sounded clear in the room of the pyramid.

" Buffaloes know that area better than we do, Brother Horse. They always stop at a water supply. We'll only have to follow their path to drink at last. “

His mount was rested. She jumped on the saddle and walked up the path of the herbivores.

This pace was suited to Black Soot. He rubbed his hands.

- Bring the kid ! He ordered.

The little animal was pushed. When one of the assistants wanted to lay him on the slab, he struggled and bit his wrist. Likewise, he planted his teeth in Black De Soot's palm, triggering the fury of the sorcerer. In rage, the master of the mound kicking the back of his nearest help. The sixty semi-human creatures who made up the audience chuckled with pleasure. The rejoicings continued !

A pig-like being approached. He held the silver tray at arm's length, and the obsidian blade on top of it.

Black Soot lifted both hands and began a sordid litany.

Fascinated by the voice of the sorcerer, the audience did not perceive the instinctive movement of Little Daisy. A sudden pain had bite her skin from the first words of the magic ritual. She had put her hand on the pendant. The medallion was tepid, a strange vibration palpitated in its ribs. This feeling disappeared quickly.

Disconcerted, the first gesture of Little Daisy was to throw this jewel for the least singular. Then she changed her mind. The medallion had regained an ordinary temperature, no vibration no longer crossed it. She shrugged her shoulders. She had dreamed without a doubt. Sometimes, the thirst was strangely affecting the senses. In his tribe, it was reported that a man lacking water could create the perfect illusion of a river. Better to concentrate on the track !

She passed a group of large rocks. Nearby, the grass had not been trampled. The bison had bypassed the hillock. Like a torrent, the herd had split into two branches and had flowed on each side. For a moment she wanted to climb up the rocks to see the animals, then gave up.

What is the use of wasting time and energy ? The bison were ahead, even though they were still too far to distinguish them.

In the pyramid, the obsidian blade dropped abruptly. Instantly, the medallion warmed to white.

Little Daisy jumped in shock. When she was back at home, she thought, she would study the jewel more. There must have been a reason for these abrupt changes in temperature.

All in her thoughts, it took her some time before noticing the silence that weighed in the air.

The same silence that which hovered over his village petrified by Black Soot. Would the sorcerer be in the neighborhood ? Eye of Toad must have been home for several days already and had informed his master of her existence and her mission. Did the sorcerer pursue her ?

These lugubrious reflections were interrupted by a vibration in the ground.

It was almost imperceptible, but in the silence reigning at that moment, Little Daisy felt it intensely. She jumped down from her horse and glued her ear to the dry land covered with crushed stems.

The vibration reached her whole body. It grew rapidly to look like a rumbling. She raised her head, wide-eyed. Five hundred yards away, a cloud of dust rose like a gray smoke.

- The buffaloes ! She shouted at last. They are rushing straight on us.

The most dreadful danger of the prairie after the fire was the charge of the buffaloes. Each flock had several tens of thousands of animals.

When panic or anger gained them, they would run without worrying about the smaller animals in front of their hoofs. They formed an invincible wall which squashed anyone who was too slow to slip away.

Jumping on the back of her horse, Little Daisy looked round. Far away, from her left to her right, stretched a black line of monstrous heads surmounted by aggressive horns. No possibility of escaping them from the sides, all that remained was the flight ahead.

She pulled the reins, forcing her steed to a sudden about-turn.

- Yeah ! Brother Horse ! Save your life and mine !

Belly on the ground, he galloped on the broad strip of grass previously crushed by the buffaloes. Little Daisy encouraged him while curling up to offer less resistance to the wind. The rumbling of the hoofs had become deafening. Already, scrolls of dust outrun them. She screamed in the din.

"Quick, brother horse ! Quick ! We have almost reached the rocks."

Almost, but not yet ! The buffaloes were only twenty yards behind them, every tenth of a second the distance was reducing. A glance back wiped out the little Inikawas. The animals were enormous. Each of them, three times bigger than his horse. They would smashed them to pieces in no time !

The wind blew harder. The cloud of dust covered the track far ahead.

Little Daisy could hardly see and his hearing was saturated with the formidable hoof pounding a few meters behind.

In a moment, the bison would be on them. The group of rocks suddenly raised its ghostly outlines in the thick cloud. In an ultimate effort, she pushed her horse there and glued it behind the eminence, against the stone.

She had not laid a boot on the ground that the whole herd of buffaloes swept across in an unbelievable tumult.

At the heart of the pyramid, a shriek of joy shook the walls of the crypt. The homunculus imitated their master. On the oval mirror, the sun had disappeared. From the great prairie there remained only the grayish dust of the dust and the frightful roar of thousands of hoofs.

* * *

The sorcerer uttered a new squeal of joy. He had seen the flock catch up with Little Daisy and flooded her. True, he had not seen the buffaloes crushing her, the cloud of dust was far too dense, but the end of the last Inikawas had no doubtful. He had paid no attention to the slightly darker masses that were carved out of the gray of the dust, so he did not suspect their possible protection. Therefore, he had good reason to think that she had been smashed under the thousand hooves of the monstrous herbivores.

Eye of Toad, anxious to regain his position as a favorite within the pyramid, launched himself into a succession of obsequious congratulations.

- Oh ! Black Soot, my master, you are the greatest ! The girl is now wiped out. She has paid her sacrilegious act and the Inikawas will remain petrified forever.

The sorcerer, sensitive to flattery like all conceited, exulted.

- You're right, gnome ! I am the tallest. No one can escape my anger wherever he finds himself.

- I am proud to serve a master like you. I hope you will grant me the privilege of organizing new festivities in your honor. Put at my disposal a score of men, I'll capture the isolated chasseurs of the neighboring tribes. I thought this night of unprecedented tortures that will enchant you.

- Later, my gnome ! The rejoicings will wait. I have to get the talisman back. It is precious, it is not known which enemy hand could pick it up.

- After the charge of the buffaloes, it must have been destroyed under their hooves !

- Undeceive yourself ! A charm protects him, he is indestructible.

He barked at the attention of the pig creature who served as an officer.

- The mirror gave me the position of the Inikawas. At her death, she was four days of ordinary ride from our base. By pressing our mounts at the most, we'll not take more than two days to arrive at the talisman. Let the horses and supply be prepared. We'll go on ride in the hour.

CHAPTER 08

Under the relentless sun

Behind the rocks, Little Daisy curled up in an anfractuosity. She had wrapped her blanket around her head. Despite this protection, the dust had infiltrated his lungs. She coughed to tear her throat. She had also covered the horse's head with the gnome's canvas. It had snorted, but she had insisted. In the end, it had let her put on him that fabric and had escaped the asphyxia.

The buffaloes had disappeared for a while. The dreadful uproar of their rush always filled the ears of Little Daisy. Her eardrums mauled did not become accustomed to silence. She had to force herself to move. The memory of dead hunters, choked by the dust resulting from a charge of buffaloes, came to her memory. The cloud would take a long time to fall. She had to leave this place veray quickly, go anywhere provided the air was cooler.

She stepped away from the rock three steps and stumbled. No way to escape it, she would have to raise her blanket from time to time to head and, as a result, swallow an additional puff of dust.

She pulled on the lanyard. The horse refused to move. He trembled. Its flanks were traversed by sporadic shocks. The poor beast was terrified. She calmed it down and pulled out again. This time her mount did not offer resistance. The canvas around her head plunged it into the darkness, yet she followed that familiar hand, that human hand that knew where to go.

For the moment, Little Daisy was only sure of one thing: the position of the setting sun. So she progressed in that direction. One step after the other, she drove her horse out of the cloud of dust. He seemed to walk for hours on end. Time had ceased to exist. When the air became breathable, the sun shone brightly. It was only halfway through his daily run.

A grin twisted the face of Little Daisy. A cough convulsed her. She spat dust through her nose, through her mouth and thought she was dying on the spot. Her solid constitution set her back on her feet. Despite her thinness, she was surprisingly resistant.

The horse was also in a pitiful condition. She cleaned her nostrils and felt that it was incapable of going any other way than walking.

- Courage, Brother Horse ! We shall soon find a stream where we shall wash ourselves of this dirt.

She spoke more to reassure herself. Water points in this area were rare. Provided she locates one before the end of the day !

She continued her journey with little steps, always towards the west. The mountain became clearer. The higher and more massive a mountain was, the more the sources there were, usely said her people. As a consequence, that one which rose in the distance had certainly water in abundance.

The West Mountains were, however, very distant. She would never reach them by wandering thus in this relentless sun. Her only one hope was to discover a stream somewhere on the prairie.

This hope sustained her all day long. In the evening, the land that lay before her was drier than ever. The height of the grass had reduced. Scattered, they now reached her shoulders. Her throat was on fire, she would have given anything for a sip of water.

She tore a handful of grass and chewed them. The stems, like dry wood, cracked under her teeth. They released only tiny drops of sap. This viscid fluid did not quench her thirst. On the contrary, he fanned it by sticking to his tongue. She would have spit it out if she had had enough saliva.

She needed water !

A moment distracted by the falling evening, she immediately recovered herself. It did not matter if it was dark, she had to go on. If she stopped now, the next day she might not have the courage or strength to get up. Moreover, the freshness would facilitate her advance.

The moon lit up her steps. Nevertheless, she stumbled frequently because of the incredible tiredness that clung to her legs. Each muscle of her body ordered her to sleep, her tongue filled all her mouth. She no longer dared to speak for fear of being unable to close her jaws again. She contented herself with pulling the horse by the halter. The animal, as exhausted as its mistress, had adopted her cadence.

There was no rivers during their gruelling march in the heart of the night. The dawn lit up a barren ground. The grasses were sunk, burnt. Evident signs that no water point would be revealed before long.

She raised her head to the mountain. Although closer now, she could scarcely distinguish it. Her eyes, wounded by the dust, the sun and the thirst, just managed to land a few steps in front of her. She sensed the presence of the massif and clenched her teeth. She would go to it, because it was her duty, because her family would remain petrified forever if she failed. Because it was their last chance to move again, to feel their heart beating and to hug their loved ones.

Her mind fixed on this resolution, she went back to her destination.

The hours passed, endless. The summer sun shone without ceasing, a real torture for the one who advanced slowly, sometimes stumbling. Her long brown hair hung down on her back and on her chest. Her thin face was nothing more than a mask of suffering, shriveled by the lack of water. And yet the little Inikawas was still walking. Sustained by her own will, she put one foot in front of the other and approached little by little the mountain.

The burning sun had accomplished two-thirds of its way when Little Daisy' foot struck against a large stone. She could not catch up and collapsed on the ground. Laboriously, she sat back on her knees. Her mount threw a plaintive neighing and went forth. She always held the halter. The sudden departure of the horse unbalanced her. She fell back into the dust and clenched the bridle firmly.

The horse took the bit between its teeth. He began to gallop, dragging his mistress behind him. Little Daisy's shoulder hit another stone. The pain made her let go. Before sinking into unconsciousness, she heard the hoofs move away.

The world was only a night devoid of sensations. Suddenly a neighing tore the darkness. The conscience returned to Little Daisy, and with it the pain. A dragon of fire burnt her throat and stomach. She did not even have the strength to groan and wished she was left in peace. A second neighing sounded. Frozen points struck her face. Again, a neigh; Then she was jostled.

Her eyes opened to close immediately. The brilliance of the sun was unbearable. A bit of understanding crossed her mind. Brother Horse had come back, he was pushing her with its head and its skins was dripping.

He had found water. It was his odor that had spurred him and caused his sudden departure.

She gathered her last strength and managed in extremis to clim in the saddle. Her tongue swollen with thirst did not allow her to speak, but the horse had understood. It moved away without the slightest gesture of the girl. Lying on the neck of her mount, Little Daisy saw nothing, heard nothing, perceiving only vaguely the movement of the horse.

The song of a stream revived her enough to give her the strength to step down. She lay down in the stream, about twenty inches deep, with her cheek on the bank. Though on the brink of inanition, her coolness did not falter. She remembered, as in a mist, the gestures to be accomplished in her situation. Above all, do not drink to satiety !

Struggling against her mouth, she succeeded in absorbing only a some drops and then waiting one minute before the other ones, then another minute before a third bunch of littles drops. When she estimated her body re-adapted to freshness and water, she drank more, and then stretched out on the shore. Sleep fell on her at one blow. Until the morning she slept like that, her feet near the water.

It was hunger that eventually drew her from her improvised bed. Her stomach clenched on scents of food he remembered. She had not eaten for two days, and the last meal had been more than light.

She still drank long bursts of clear water and filled her leather flask. The horse was grazing . He was fresh and ready. The two days of drought had not impressed upon him any apparent traces.

"It's time to eat for me too," murmured Little Daisy.

She thanked her horse to takke her to the stream. The horse neighed. He pawed the groung with impatience.

- You seem to have overcome this painful adventure. Do not worry, we'll leave as soon as I have eaten.

Many thick bushes scattered on the bank. Their juicy fruits offered the comfort of a sweet pulp. She picked as many as she could and packed a certain amount for her next meal.

A little later, washed and rested, she mounted in the saddle. She had lost her eagle feather. Only the typical headband of his tribe retained her hair. She smoothed them with her hand and said to steed.

" Forward, Brother Horse ! " The West Mountains are waiting for us.

The horse asked only to trot. She let it go at his own pace.

The mountain was terribly close now. Little Daisy looked up at its imposing mass. She had never seen such a high land. She gazed the fine point which surmounted the whole. There was the Sun Stone, on the other side, that one exposed to the sunset.

In the middle of the day, Little Daisy approached the base of the mountain. She studied it attentively. At the level of the plain, the slope was relatively soft. At mid-height, it stiffened to become very steep. Some crevices cut the massif in places. She guessed their presence to the differences in luminosity, to the shadows areas visibles from her position.

The hour of truth approached, she reached the end of her quest.

She jumped at the bottom of her horse and talked it a little moved.

- Our road ends here, Brother Horse. I can not take you further, you do not know how to climb. And I do not know how long I would take to find the Sun Stone. Maybe one day, maybe more. And at that moment, I still have to wait until sunset to pick it up. Until then, you could die of thirst. So I give you your freedom.

She removed the saddle and the bridle. The horse seemed surprised.

- Yes ! You are free now. Go where you want !

She put her bag on her shoulders. It always contained its starting equipment. Except for his missing feather, bow and quiver lost during the charge of the buffaloes, her bag and things inside were teh same than the first day of her expedition. Her hair floated freely to his waist. Her knife was shining on his belt. His left hand secured his fastening while the right stood on her tomahawk.

- I'm ready for the last stage, she exclaimed. Sister Mountain, Little Daisy visits you !

On these enthusiastic words, she leapt on the rocky slope. She turned again.

- Good-bye, Brother Horse ! Go your way.

The animal saluted his departure. He reared on his hind legs and uttered a neighing before moving away at a gallop.

Little Daisy gave him a big smile and began climbing the mountain.

CHAPTER 09

The West Mountains

At that very moment, a howl of rage resounded in the plain about forty kilometers away. Black Soot had just discovered, near a heap of rocks, the traces of the hooves of a horse and those of small boots. The footprints stood out with great clarity in the dust covering the mown grass.

- She-demone ! She got away.

His anger was such that he struck the creature closest to him. Half humane, like all the wizard's servants, this one looked like a man to whom a jackal's head had been placed. The blow of his master sent him to the bottom of his horse.

Seeing that his followers remained fearfully aloof, Black Soot roared.

- Miserable pigs! Have you searched around ?

He knew the answers in advance. For thirty minutes they had beaten the neighborhood without finding anything but these footprints. The traces indicated that the little Inikawas had taken refuge behind a rock with her horse before moving away. Obviously she had kept the talisman. He thought quickly. She was without water, he had heard her complain about that before he started the buffaloes attack. Its progression had therefore been very limited. Perhaps she lay lifeless somewhere, not more far than hundred flights of arrows from here or a thousand. Raking blindly around was not a good idea since he could find the girl by otherwise more effective means.

His knowledge of witchcraft was sufficiently advanced to locate the talisman wherever he may be. He could have accomplished the ritual here. However, far from the pyramid, this action would have cost him a lot of energy and would have weakened it. He had too many enemies in the great meadow to allow himself the least softening.

His evil spirit conceived a new project. How had he not thought of it earlier ?

The most serious danger came from Mother of the Tibe, the dean of the Inikawas. In possession of the talisman, she would fight him. She was not, therefore, to escape from her immobility. To do this, it was enough to destroy the sole element capable of defeating his spell : the Sun Stone. These crystals existed only on the West Mountains, as Little Daisy used to say. It was absolutely necessary to crush them, to smash them to the last. He would thus definitely deprive the Inikawas, as well as any other of his enemies, of any possibility of rejecting his mystical force.

As for Little Daisy, she was physically vulnerable. If his magic fluid was inert against the talisman, it was not the same about the real weapons. A simple arrow would put an end to her existence.

He spat an order, and the column galloped

towards the West Mountains. Before, he took care to warn his troop.

- Open your eyes, wretched bipeds ! The first one of you who sees the girl will have the privilege of sticking her dagger into her heart.

The grotesque monkeys or pigs screamed their approval. During the next ride, they scrutinized the prairie intensely, eager to strike the first blow. Since the wizard had transformed them into human caricatures, they hated every man, woman or child normally constituted. And the torments they could inflict on them rejoiced them to the point of disgust.

While the bloodthirsty troops were rushing down to the mountain, Little Daisy began to climb the base of the massif. The smooth slope of the first fifty meters gradually stiffened. She did not care. The end of his mission was approaching, sweeping away her tiredness. Her muscles worked wonderfully, as if they had never experienced the trying walk of the last three days. Such vigour flowed in her being that she was almost astonished.

The light breeze brought the echo of a distant growl.

Little Daisy stopped suddenly. She had never heard somethig like that before. It looked like that one of the cougar, a wild beast living in the high plateaus. She had never encountered them, however, during the tales of the hunt, men of the tribe had often imitated her cry. The sounds which had just come to her evoked singularly the imitations of the storytellers.

A worried gleam burned her wide dark eyes. The hunters reported that the cougar did not attack humans, but fled from them. Opposed to a little girl, alone and defenseless, would it act the same ? Her hand went down on her tomahawk and she rectified : " Not defenseless ! " According to the descriptions she remembered, a cougar on her paws came only at the height of the belt of an adult man. It was not a real great threat. Brother Tomahawk would give her the advantage in case of an attack !

This reflection comforted her. She sent a

friendly thought to her favorite weapon and resumed the ascent.

The eastern slope of the mountain was now very steep. Sometimes she had to kneel down to pass a difficult corridor. Her skirt of leather clung in bushes with particularly sharp thorns. Here and there her garment was lacerated. It allowed glimpses of gashes.

Little Daisy sacrificed his blanket. She cut out two large strips of solid fabric. Shortly afterwards, she had formed two legs, very acceptable and resistant to the hardest of thorns. She held them on her thighs with a piece of rope.

Thus protected, she rose, proud of her invention.

Sisters Thorns could well attack her skirt, they would no longer hurt her legs. This shield was also useful to her against the sharp edges of the rock. She was ignorant of the mountains, so more than once a stone had been went out under her feet, causing her to stumble. Without the protection of her leggings, she would have had her knees in blood for a long time.

Canyons were spliting the massif at the most unexpected moment. Their configuration was complex. She did not detect them until the last moment. From then on, he had to enter into this narrow ravine to continue her climbing a little further. This, after having meandered through a maze of rocks, thorn bushes and shrunken shrubs to the point that they were believed dead.

Tirelessly, however, she climbed up.

Halfway down, Little Daisy had a break. Examining the summit of the mountain, she drank a bit. The freshness of the water revived her. Thrifty, she drank only three sips. She studied the summit again. It was close now ! The climbing of this latter part would be more difficult than the first. The slopes were steeper.

A growl ragged her out from her meditation. Stronger than the previous one, it announced the presence of the wild beast in the neighborhood.

Better to move away from it.

She adjusted her bag on her shoulders when a series of shrieks suddenly rang. They came from the canyon opened on her right. She engaged cautiously, though without excessive fear. The scream had resumed. They were more of a bird than of a cougar.

Twenty steps, a rock to get round, and suddenly ... The little Inikawas froze on the spot, an expression of intense surprise on the face.

Beating frantically on the wings, an immense condor was shouting sharply stridulations. The mouth of the young climber roundered, her eyes widened. With the wings spread, the bird blocked the entire canyon. It exceeded the four meters of wingspan. Compares with it, the protective totem of the Inikawas was only a pale representation. Little Daisy understood the reason why his people had adopted the condor as their emblem. The giant bird was of incredible majesty.

A terrible roar broke her contemplation. She

turned back quickly to discover a picture even more amazing.

Fifty yards away, a gigantic beast clung to the top of a rock. Despite the distance, Little Daisy felt the power of the muscles under the fawn-colored skin streaked with black. A saber-toothed tiger ! Their species was believed to have been extinct for more than a century, exterminated by the hunters of Atlantis. The savagery of these wild beasts had made it a game of choice for this people as barbarous as the animal. They had come in large numbers, armed with javelins of fire killing at a distance and had finally eliminated them in their entirety. Some of them had certainly escaped, and the one who had sprung from the stones testified.

The claws of the tiger hung the hard rock. His fangs were twice as long as the arms of Little Daisy, his jaws would have crushed his head with a single bite. However, the deadly bundles of yellow eyes did not see her. They twisted in those of the condor.

For a moment, time stopped. Then the bird

cackled and clawed the stone of one of his talons. The saber-toothed tiger gathered. The muscles of his body contracted. He was going to jump.

"But what is he waiting for to fly ?" She exasperated.

As soon as her question was asked, she knew the answer. One of the condor's legs was trapped in an anfractuosity. He found himself stuck to the ground. Its dreadful beak would not repel the predator for a very long time.

The saber-toothed tiger was the most terrifying carnivore she'd ever met. Larger than the condor, it measured about five meters in length and two meters in height. No known animal could have resisted him, not even a buffalo !

In the near future, the proud condor would be nothing more than a shredded flesh.

A revolt rumbled in the heart of Little Daisy. She could not let the tiger devour the emblem of her tribe. He was the protector of the Inikawas, they had to defend it, even at the cost of thier lives !

Before the wild beast bounded, she threw a stone at him, uttering a loud cry. This unexpected intrusion surprised the tiger. He turned his yellow eyes toward her and gauged her with a cold intelligence. She trembled in terror. On a reflex, she had stepped in and now she had to face the incredible monster. It swung his head, from the condor to the girl, from the girl to the condor. Finally, his choice was on the weakest of the two : Little Daisy. True, she was smaller than the condor, but, unlike the bird, she had neither beaks nor talons likely to hurt it. In addition, she would make a meal quite acceptable.

He leaped to the bottom of his rock and examined his prey.

The hand of Little Daisy had closed on his tomahawk as soon as the tiger appeared. When he was on the ground, at her level, she noticed the futility of her defense. The head of the beast was higher than her, its legs were as wide as its own chest. She would never have enough length to strike a vital center, not to mention the leather of the animal, as thick as that of a buffalo. Her tomahawk would scratch it, while the claw back would tear her up and down.

The sharp spirit of the hunter vibrated in the head of Little Daisy. If force was in her disfavor, cunning would compensate her. The tricks of generations of Inikawas warriors cropped up. She knew what to do.

His tomahawk mowed the big branch of a shrub to his right. His lighter lit a tiny flame.

The tiger approached slowly, with faint feet. His prey was defenseless and it knew it. She could not escape either. Her smell, however, was foreign to it, and she spread a suspicious perfume. His eyes settled on the drop of fire that was gaining momentum. An odor of ash tickled his muzzle. He tetanized at once and groaned nervously.

The delicate young prey approached him boldly, the drop of fire in her hand. He stared at her, worried.

- Go away ! Brother Tiger. Leave us alone !

Little Daisy waved the inflamed branch. The tiger rolled up his chops and growled..

- Go away ! She ordered again. If not, Brother Fire will burn you to the marrow !

She pretended to throw the branch on him. The tiger leaps back. This movement fills the little Inikawas with joy.

The beast reacted like all animals, it feared an only one enemy : fire! Armed with courage, she advanced step by step, shouting it loudly to withdraw while swinging the branch at arm's length. And the tiger retreated. With one stroke of his paw, he could have swept the girl and the brandon, but the fear of fire prevailed. His mind was inaccessible to logical reasoning.

In a last roar of anger and fright, he abandoned the game. The most formidable beast of the continent flees before the determination of a little girl.

Little Daisy turned to the condor. He had

neither moved nor emitted sounds, seemingly suspended from the anguish of the confrontation. His intelligent eyes probed the girl.

- He has run away, Brother condor. He will not come back, anyway, any time soon. We'll have plenty of time to leave this canyon.

The condor nodded as if he understood. Then he shook his head and cracked weakly. Little Daisy understood the meaning of his appeal.

- You are a prisoner ! You will not be able to leave, will you ?

The bird said nothing. The little Inikawas put her brand at some distance - even the condors were afraid of the fire.

- Do not be afraid, Brother Condor, I'm going to rescue you. Just let me get close to you, I do not want you any harm.

He did not flinch, just watching her walk towards him. She was impressed. The talons of the gigantic bird could have enclosed her as easily as a newborn in the hands of an adult.

His right leg had slipped into a crevice so that he could only extract it by making the same gestures upside down. This, of course, was beyond his faculties. She therefore set out to break the trap.

His tomahawk hacked the rock around his paw. Soon the bird was able to disengage completely. He flew so abruptly that the breath of his fluttering wings disturbed the balance of his liberator. He spun for a moment over her, shrieking sharply before moving away at a dizzying pace.

- Bye, Brother Condor ! Shouted out Little Daisy.

But the condor could no longer hear her. He was no more than a black spot in the sky.

CHAPTER 10

The Sun Stone

The climbing of the last section of the mountain was particularly harsh. The skirt of Little Daisy was no more than a rag and her hands scratched everywhere. She now progressed almost continuously on all fours. The slope was too vertical to allow her to walk.

Shortly before reaching the summit, she walked round the massif, now like a large peak.

The vision she discovered caught a movement of surprise. A little higher, on a narrow and slightly inclined terrace stretched tens of crystals, the size of a fist. They shone with incomparable brilliance. At the present moment, they threw the orange fires of the setting sun.

- The Sunstone !

The cry of Little Daisy rang out all over the mountain. He cascaded down on the flanks of the massif, reverberated in the surrounding meadow and shook a tall man dressed in black riding a horse color at night.

- La Pierre De Soleil, she exclaimed again.

She rushed forward, covering the last area separating her from the terrace, half crawling over the hard, steep rock. The sun was declining.

Soon it would be red. If she did not pick the stone now, she would have to wait another twenty-four hours. With the saber-toothed tiger lurking in the mountain, she could not take the risk.

She reached the terrace even as the sky dyed a dazzling red.

This shade lasted only a short time, but Little Daisy no longer cared about. In the palm of his hand was a ruby of a fabulous brilliancy and purity.

The fires he threw were identical to those which the sun had projected for a quarter of a second. Now the horizon, though red, was slowly losing its brightness. The Sunstones, uncollected, followed the change of color of the diurnal star. Their dark red color darkened. In a short time they would be as black as the night.

At the foot of the mountain, Black Soot was fulminating.

Little Daisy's scream of joy had made him rage. At the very moment when she had picked up the Sun Stone, he had known it. A sort of instinct had warned him, unleashing in him a wave of terror. He had to annihilate her now, otherwise it would be too late !

His finger pointed to the nearest pig-like creature.

- Tie up it and hold it tight on the ground !

The half-human squealed horribly and tried to escape. Eye of Toad toppled him treacherously, then, laughing, watched the rush of his companions. In a jiffy, the fugitive found himself tied to the feet of Black Soot. He struggled with the terror of the condemned man. The sorcerer, kicked in the shin, roared with pain. Another creature, half man, half a cock, laughed nervously when he saw his terrible master skip on one leg. Black Soot glared at him, promising himself to chastise the impudent man on his return.

- Wretched swine ! Do you want to stop agitating. It's your master who commands it !

The porcine being was twitching more and more. He held up the sorcerer to redicule in front of his own troop. Black Soot barked.

Two others of his servants left the ranks to hold the prisoner. Their hilarious expression did not escape to their master, increasing his fury. However, he mastered himself. Before taking care of the discipline of his troop, he had to eliminate his enemy.

He began his horrible ritual in a hoarse voice. So near his victim, he did not need to see her to cast on her the dark forces of his vindictiveness. The blade of obsidian plunged into the heart of the sacrificed creature, causing a sudden heat of the medallion around the neck of Little Daisy.

* * *

She gasped. The burning of the pendant had broken the rapture that was bathing her. She touched the metal, it was heated to white. Before she could remove it, a roar shook the crystals.

The saber-toothed tiger had just emerged, tremendous, terrible with savagery. His jaws were like traps with spears, his eyes thundering with wild flashes.

Little Daisy stood up immediately. She moved back a step. The tiger approached. She waved the ruby at arm's length. His brilliance illuminated the terrace. The fawn hesitated, she took advantage of it to climb a little more towards the summit.

The wider pupils of the feline fixed the ruby, wondering about its danger.

A flash of understanding crossed the spirit of Little Daisy while his hand accidentally clashed with the still hot medallion. The words of the gnome came back to him. The medallion belonged to his master, Black Soot. It had heated just before each of the sudden attacks of the animals of the great prairie against her. There was no doubt that the sorcerer was behind all this. One way or another, the medallion was magic ! What use could it bring him against the tiger ?

The beast did not give her time for reflection. It opened a jaw like a chasm and jumped onto the terrace. The ruby had no smell or sound, it was not dangerous. The little Inikawas read her end in the yellow eyes of the tiger. Her right hand looked desperately for her tomahawk, she could not clear it.

The scene seemed to slow down. In reality, everything went so fast that one could hardly distinguish each movement. Little Daisy recorded the vision of a fawn coat propelled towards her by muscles of an inconceivable power. His hearing captured a growl of victory only one hundredth of a second before an unbelievable noisiness of the air.

Fangs like daggers, longer than his head, shone

before his eyes before disappearing completely, replaced by a dark red sky. And she went up, went upstairs ... The tiger beneath her was writhing with rage.

She felt the grip around her waist and shoulders and understood. A glance above her confirmed her. The condor had taken her away, just as the saber-toothed tiger leapt over her.

- Thank you, Brother Condor ! You saved my life.

Her happiness was such that she forgot her uncomfortable situation. The condor flew over the summit of the mountain, and went down to the great prairie on the other side. A howl of pure fury whipped him. He beat his wings, suspicious, not knowing what danger lay on the ground. He did not dare to land and circled.

Two hundred yards below him, a tall man on a black horse, his head thrown back, vociferated like a lunatic.

- Black Soo ! Souted Little Daisy.

She had never seen him, but the two lakes of hatred which the eyes of the unknown man projected to her were amply sufficient to inform her of his identity. The presence of the gnome at his side certified it.

The sorcerer was in a black rage as terrible as the fear that gripped him. For the first time in his life he trembled. Drops of sweat ran down his chin, his knees were flailing. He could not took off his gaze from the Sunstone, bursting with light, held by the little girl. She was going to succeed, and he would be defeated.

Terror filled him. He uttered a howl of madness. That would not be! He clasped both hands. At the moment they came in contact, a tongue of fire gushed up, flashing towards the condor.

Little Daisy guessed the sorcerer's intentions as soon as his arms had risen. An impulse guided his fingers. She snatched the medallion from her neck and waved it forward. The fire line bounces off the talisman and returns twice as fast to its point of emission. Black Soot had no time to sketch anything. His mystical ray struck him in return and petrified him and his troop into absolute immobility.

* * *

The condor, disconcerted, turned over the scene of the drama. Little Daisy had the leisure to examine the column. All the wizard's servants were turned into stone. Black Soot himself was no more than a harmless statue. She remembered her tribe. Her own were stiffened and Mother Of The Tribe was waiting for her.

A weird idea came to her suddenly. It was only an intuition, but why not try ? She streched her hand to the condor's chest. By dint of small blows, she put an end to his whirling and headed east.

The impressions she kept of that night were fabulous. It flew high in the sky, at a phenomenal speed. For the gigantic wings of the great condor, her weight was negligible. He split the air ten times faster than any horse. The wind rumbled in the hair of Little Daisy. The prairie waved more than ever under the light of the moon. The ruby well sheltered in her tunic and pressed against her heart, she melted into this enchantment.

At dawn, she recognized her village with the totem in the middle of it. She pulled the condor's leg down several times. The great bird understood what she wanted. He landed smoothly at the entrance of the village, then flew away

- Bye, Brother Cndor ! She whispered.

The beak upside down, he made a shrill crack and flew faster than an arrow of hunters. She immediately rushed through the tepees towards the central square. The men, women and children were still there, in the same position as two weeks before, when she had left them.

She took off the ruby. It sparkled with red and shone with a thousand fires. She tore herself away from the delight of her contemplation and placed it in the hand of Mother of the Tribe. The old woman's stone fingers softened, then her arms. The whole body finally became animated and her eyelids opened.

- Mother of the Tribe, I bring you the Sun Stone, cried Little Daisy suddenly moved.

Tears of joy in her eyes, the dean of the Inikawas struggled to answer.

- You succeeded, Little Daisy ! I was sure. You are the bravest in our village. Never will your name be erased from the memory of the Inikawas.

She stood up and took her by the arm.

- Come, now, let us put the Sun Stone on each of us, let's wake up the village !

* * *

Seeing the members of his tribe come out one after the other from their rigidity, the girl's heart leaped with joy.

A bright smile flourished on her luminous face in an opaline corolla. Never as much as on that day did she look so like a wonderful Little Flower of the Fields, a wonderful Little Daisy !

End

Other books of Patrick Huet

Fantasy. Adult, **Young adult and Teen.**

* Sequana the legend of the Seine.

***Little Daisy series*:**

- The Sun Stone.
- The Pearl of the Moon.
- The Cristal of Light.

Tales for children.

Tomy's series (for children)

- Tomy the little magician and the key of the bedroom.
- Tomy at the zoo.
- Tomy and the diamond ring.
- Tomy at the North pole.
- Tomy and the baby pigeon.
- Tomy and the learned fleas.

More informations on www.patrickhuet.net

www.ingramcontent.com/pod-product-compliance
Ingram Content Group UK Ltd.
Pitfield, Milton Keynes, MK11 3LW, UK
UKHW021051270726
13967UKWH00012B/546